PRAISE FOR DAEDALUS COMBAT

Daedalus Combat is a fitting conclusion to and culmination of the other three stories in Williscroft's action-packed, hard science-fiction series, *The SWIC Daedalus Files*. When Pirates snatch a U.S. Senator and probable next President from a ship and hold him for one hundred million dollars ransom, the Navy SEALS quickly move to rescue him. Once again Derek "Tiger" Baily's six-man SWIC squad is featured, only this time, the operation is "dramatically different from anything any warrior had ever done before." Why? Because it's the first time anyone has ever "dropped from LEO [Low Earth Orbit] into a combat scenario."

It's the full nature of this combat scenario that is the real "Wow" factor here. All the different units of the military machine must work together if the mission is to succeed. The action and suspense are intense, and they kept me turning the pages until the very end.

— Professor John B. Rosenman, Norfolk State University
Former Chairman of the Board, Horror Writers Association
Author of *The Inspector of the Cross Series*

The test and training runs are over; now it's time for the SWIC to see real action. Williscroft's latest, *Daedalus Combat*, literally starts with a bang and keeps on going...

— Alastair Mayer
Author of *The T-Space Series*

This final short story by author Robert Williscroft brings Lt. Cdr. Derek "Tiger" Baily into a rescue mission with no margin for error. Sporting the newest version of the fully-armed wingsuit (the Gryphon 10 Mk 4), Tiger and his squad must rescue a U.S. Senator—and presumed future President—who is being held for ransom by pirates.

Each of the *Daedalus* adventures, told through the voice of Tiger, is a short story, and I'd encourage fans of sci-fi and military thrillers to read them in the order they were published—they stitch together smoothly into a comprehensive tale of adventure and suspense. In *Daedalus Combat*, author Williscroft demonstrates his knowledge of military tactics and equipment to paint an all-too-realistic picture of what could be tomorrow's headlines. This is an exciting, hard-charging read that is sure to satisfy thriller and sci-fi readers.

— Dr. Dave Edlund
***USA Today* Bestselling Author –**
The Peter Savage Thrillers

Clandestine military operations depend on the element of surprise; Navy SEALS fast-roping from a helicopter, or exiting a submarine in the middle of the night. But the ultimate surprise would be dropping a combat team on an unsuspecting enemy from low earth orbit (LEO). Not LEO of a spaceship, or spaceplane, but of actual combatants, living, breathing human beings, armed to the teeth, crossing oceans in minutes, and pouncing as a team of flying, fire-breathing dragons.

Who would have thought?

Well, that's exactly the point. No one would...except Navy SEAL "Tiger" Bailey, Commanding Officer of SEALS Winged Insertion Command Three (SWIC-3).

Robert Williscroft places you inside the action, inside the incredible space launches, the orbital rendezvous, the almost flaming reentry, the on-the-fly change of plans, attack under hellacious conditions, and egress from the combat scene.

Like any combat operation, there are risks at every step of the way, and Williscroft brings you, the reader, along for the ride of a lifetime.

At the end of this short read you'll breathe a sigh of relief, let out a little cheer for our unsung heroes, and then wonder—could this really happen? Don't ask this reviewer. I'm sworn to secrecy.

— Dr. John R. Clarke
Author of *The Jason Parker Series*

DAEDALUS COMBAT

SWIC Combat Drop from Low Earth Orbit

DAEDALUS COMBAT

SWIC Combat Drop from Low Earth Orbit

Robert G. Williscroft

Guntersville

Daedalus Combat:
SWIC Combat Drop from Low Earth Orbit

Fresh Ink Group
An Imprint of:
The Fresh Ink Group, LLC
1021 Blount Avenue, #931
Guntersville, AL 35976
Email: info@FreshInkGroup.com
FreshInkGroup.com

Edition 1.0 2019

Images by Robert G. Williscroft
Book design by Amit Dey / FIG
Cover design by Stephen Geez / FIG
Associate publisher Lauren A. Smith / FIG

Keywords: Airlock, Amelia Earhart Skyport, Baker Island, Fred Noonan Skyport, Free Fall, Gryphon, Hawaii, Houston, Howland Island, Hypergolic, Jarvis Island, Kiritimati Island, Launch Loop, NASA, San Diego, Space Suit, Wingsuit

Cataloging-in-Publication Recommendations:
FIC028020 FICTION / Science Fiction / Hard Science Fiction
FIC002000 FICTION / Action & Adventure
FIC028010 FICTION / Science Fiction / Action & Adventure

Library of Congress Control Number: 2019915669

ISBN-13: 978-1-947867-65-9 Papercover
ISBN-13: 978-1-947867-66-6 Hardcover
ISBN-13: 978-1-947867-67-3 Ebooks

DEDICATION

*This story is dedicated to all of the Teams,
all of the U.S. Navy SEALS, who put our safety
ahead of theirs world-wide.*

TABLE OF CONTENTS

ACKNOWLEDGEMENTS

Several people contributed to the creation of this series.

Most significantly, my wonderful wife, Jill, whom I first met when I returned from a year at the South Pole conducting atmospheric research, and who finally consented to marry me nearly thirty years later, pored over this story with her discerning engineer's eye. She kept my timeline honest and made sure that regular readers could understand fully the arcane details of the Launch Loop and the Gryphon.

Hard science fiction authors Alastair Mayer, John Clarke, and Prof John Rosenman, and USA Today bestselling author Dave Edlund reviewed the manuscript and offered their editorial insights.

Lauren Smith from Fresh Ink Group applied her professional associate publisher's eye to improve the story.

It goes without saying that any remaining omissions, errors, and mistakes fall directly on my shoulders.

Robert G. Williscroft, PhD
Centennial, Colorado
October 2019

FOREWORD

Slingshot is my novel about constructing the world's first Space Launch Loop. The book was launched August, 2015, at the International Space Elevator Conference in Seattle, and resides on the desk of every Space Elevator scientist in the world. Space Launch Loops appear in the subsequent books in *The Starchild Trilogy*, and anyone familiar with my *Trilogy* knows all about these commercial space launch systems.

When I discovered the *Gryphon* rigid wingsuit, the *SWIC Daedalus Files* stories pushed themselves into my consciousness. The first story, *Daedalus*, is a consequence of Slingshot's skyports effectively being 80 km tall wingsuit base-jumping towers. The second story, *Daedalus LEO*, follows naturally from the first—a drop from Low Earth Orbit (LEO). The third story, *Daedalus Squad*, is a consequence of the proof-of-concept LEO drop. In the third story, an entire SWIC squad drops from LEO together, in preparation for this final tale, an actual combat drop.

SEAL derring-do is real, the science and technology are real, the *Gryphon* rigid wingsuit is real, and I suspect that something like SWIC will become part of the U.S. Navy SEALS in the relatively near future.

Robert G. Williscroft
Centennial, Colorado
October 2019

CAST OF CHARACTERS

SEAL Winged Insertion Command (SWIC)

Navy Capt. Brad Nelson—Commanding Officer SWIC.

Lt.Cdr. Tom Spitzer—Executive Officer SWIC.

Mother—Controlling computer synchronized across each unit in an operation.

Max—Full-size *Gryphon-10* simulator

SEAL Winged Insertion Command Three (SWIC-3)

Lt.Cdr. Derek "Tiger" Baily—Narrator, Commanding Officer SWIC-3.

Navy Lt. Jim Fox—Executive Officer SWIC-3.

Master Chief Jerry Boldt—Master Chief SWIC-3.

Senior Chief Bob Baxter—Master Chief Boldt's second.

1st Squad—SWIC-3

Navy Lt. Roger "Rog" Brook—Squad Leader

Chief Douglas Slade

Petty Officer 1st Class Francisco "Jerico" Rodriguez

Petty Officer 1st Class Ronald "Cappy" Caplan

Petty Officer 2nd Class Peter "Pete" Farwall

Not participating in the drop

Petty Officer 2nd Class Benjamin "Benny" Williams

Petty Officer 2nd Class Christopher "Piggy" Pigwell

Petty Officer 3rd Class Clyde "Cowboy" Horseman

Launch Loop International (LLI)

Sam Davidson—Slingshot Director.

Apryl Searson—Chief Diver EMT.

U.S. Air Force C-130 Hercules

Lt.Col. Randal Dorsey, U.S. Air Force—C-130 Hercules pilot

U.S. Navy Aircraft Carrier Fighter Squadron

Lt. Joe "Happy" Snider–U.S. Navy fighter pilot

Lt. Bob "Borax" Johnson–U.S. Navy fighter pilot

Tasmanian Ocean Cruises

Capt. Mansur Darusman—Captain of the *CS Platypus*

Senator Jack Manfred—Wealthy scion of the American East Coast Manfred political family. Personal friend of the President and likely to be the next U.S. President.

DAEDALUS COMBAT

MOZAMBIQUE CHANNEL—200 KILOMETERS NORTHEAST OF MAYOTTE ISLAND

The explosion showered Capt. Mansur Darusman with thousands of tempered glass shards as the windscreens on the bridge of the Tasmanian Cruise Ship *CS Platypus* burst inward. Darusman slammed to the deck bleeding from dozens of cuts on face and hands, the front of his captain's uniform shredded. As he painfully raised himself to one knee, his undamaged eyes, shielded by cracked but still intact glasses, sought the source of the explosion. In good weather, he kept the weathertight doors to the flying bridges latched but not sealed. The explosion had blown both open. He got to his feet and turned to his right.

A dark-skinned man wearing a white turban-like headcloth, blue tee-shirt and khaki trousers, shod in ragged sneakers, and carrying an AK-47, stepped through the door and fired a burst of three shots, striking the captain's right arm and shoulder. Darusman dropped back to the deck as the pirate swept the bridge with his fire, killing everyone but the captain.

"Senator…senator!" the Pirate screamed, pointing his weapon at Darusman's head.

Darusman got to his feet slowly, left hand in the air, right dangling uselessly at his side.

Another pirate entered the left bridge door and pointed his weapon at the captain. He also wore a headcloth, but his tee-shirt was pink with black trousers. His sneakers were even more ragged than the first pirate's. The first pirate waved the other one down and screamed again, "Senator!

Senator!" Then he commenced pushing and prodding the captain toward a door at the back of the bridge.

"No! No!" Darusman said, trying not to sound challenging. He reached for the mike to the general announcing system and held it up in his open hand.

Both pirates pointed their weapons at his head.

"The Senator," Darusman said, waving the mike. "Senator Manfred..."

The first pirate nodded with a grin displaying several missing teeth.

Darusman pressed the General Announcing call button with his thumb, "Senator Manfred, Senator Jack Manfred, your presence is requested on the bridge. Senator Manfred, please come to the bridge." Then he surreptitiously pressed a second button on the mike. "Mayday, Mayday...Tasmanian *CS Platypus* hijacked...Mayday... Mayd..."

Both pirates fired, splattering Capt. Darusman's brains all over the bridge.

✳

A young airman in AFRICOM Mozambique headquarters intercepted a Mayday message and passed it to his supervising sergeant.

A Navy Radioman in Diego Garcia intercepted a Mayday call and passed it to his Chief-of-the-Watch.

A Radioman on a U.S. Navy cruiser patrolling the Gulf of Aden picked up a distress call and passed it to his Officer-of-the-Deck.

Within fifteen minutes a tanker aircraft was dispatched from AFRICOM Mozambique, two Navy jet fighters were scrambled from a U.S. Carrier on patrol near the Gulf of Oman, and SWIC-3 was mobilized at its newly established base on Howland Island in the equatorial Pacific.

Ten minutes after this, Lt.Col. Randal Dorsey was located on leave in Germany on a Rhein River cruise. He was picked up by helicopter from the river cruise ship, whisked to Ramstein Air Base, and from thence to a supersonic executive jet belonging to Ramstein's commanding general.

Two-and-a-half-hours later, Dorsey stepped onto the tarmac at Antsiranana International Airport on the northern tip of Madagascar...just as

SWIC-3 skipper Lt.Cdr. Derek "Tiger" Baily, with paramedic Apryl Searson and the senior five members of Squad One, arrived at Amelia Earhart Skyport eighty kilometers above Baker Island.

AMELIA EARHART SKYPORT—PRELAUNCH

I pulled myself away from Apryl and jumped out of bed to get dressed as I took an audio call from SWIC Commanding Officer Navy Capt. Brad Nelson. SWIC-3 was being mobilized, he said, and we had to get to Amelia Earhart Skyport as quickly as possible.

"I'll get the Team moving, Brad, and call you back," I told him.

I put a Link override call to Lt. Roger Brook. "Mobilize the Team," I told him. "You, Slade, Jerico, Cappy, and Pete will fly with me. Assemble a support team and meet me topside."

I called Nelson back. "Okay," I said, "we'll be ready to launch in thirty minutes or less."

"Here's the situation," Brad said. "Senator Jack Manfred..."

"The one who's likely to be the next President?" I asked, interrupting.

"The same," Brad said. "He, his wife, and daughter are on vacation in the Indian Ocean on the Tasmanian cruise ship *CS Platypus*—or I should say, *were*. *Platypus* has been hijacked in the waters north of Madagascar. We don't know much yet, but the French government tells us that pirates are operating out of Mayotte Island."

"Mayotte Island?" I had no idea where or what it was.

"Used to be a French Insular Department, like Hawaii to us, but a decade ago rebels overran the island, and France decided it was not worth recovering. Mayotte has been sustaining itself through small-time piracy."

"Looks like they graduated to the big time," I said.

"That's one way of putting it," Nelson quipped. "Your job is to rescue Senator Manfred and get the ship back."

"Lethal force?" I asked.

"Authorized," Nelson answered.

I headed out the door with Apryl in my wake.

"A couple of Navy fighters will locate *Platypus*," Nelson told me. "Dorsey will arrive at Antsiranana on the northern tip of Madagascar by the time you launch. We got him because of his previous aerial pickup experience. The Madagascar Air Force has agreed to let him fly one of their C-130s.

"We assume the pirates are taking the *Platypus* to Mayotte. It has the largest lagoon of any island. We expect them to dock at the Port of Longoni on the northern side of Mayotte. We're redirecting a surveillance satellite to get you the best possible intel. By the time you are ready to drop, we will have uploaded all the details into Mother."

Apryl and I climbed aboard a waiting Chinook and departed for Baker. We kept the *Gryphons* in ready storage on Baker to enable more rapid deployment. The Team landed at Baker a few minutes following my alert and had checked out each wingsuit by the time we arrived. Both Rog and Slade had checked my unit out, so I held off checking it myself until our arrival at the skyport.

Our capsule arrived at Amelia Earhart Skyport, tilted to horizontal, and sealed against the skyport lock. After the door opened inward, Apryl and I stepped into the reception area to join my guys.

"Everyone okay physically?" I asked.

"I got a bit of an earache," Jerico said.

Slade glowered at him, but Apryl walked over to him and inserted her otoscope into his left ear. Then she pulled it out and kissed his ear. "Is that better?" she asked to the howls of the other guys.

"I think my right ear's hurting now," Jerico said, but shut up when Slade slapped the back of his head.

✷

"This is for real, guys," I said as they formed up loosely in front of me. I told them about the *Platypus*, the pirates, the Senator, the Senator's family, and Dorsey. "Here's how we'll do it," I said. "Jerico and I will head inland on Mayotte Island to coordinates Mother will receive just before we drop and maybe even during our drop. The four of you," I indicated the others, "will take the ship, take out the pirates, and get the hell out of Dodge."

I pulled up a holoimage Nelson had sent me. "We think they will tie the ship up here." I pointed to the Longoni Container Ship Dock. "We're dropping in late night. Pete—you hit the dock and cut the mooring hawsers. Rog and Slade, you take the bridge and get the ship underway. Cappy, you take out the rest of the bad guys…lethal force is authorized—take no prisoners!"

"Hooyah!" Chief Slade said, joined by the rest. "Hooyah!"

"Pete, as soon as you can safely do so, get airborne and join Rog and the others." I stopped to let the instructions sink in. "We know they got small arms. Don't know about shoulder-launched missiles. You know that we added rear-facing energy-beam weapons to each *Mark five Gryphon*. Mother should be able to take out anything fired at your rear." I stopped and looked each guy in his eyes. "Rog, you and Slade gonna have to get the *Platypus* from Mayotte to Antsiranana on Madagascar. We'll send you a pilot to dock it, and will try to get him on board sooner if possible." I looked around. "Any questions?" I asked.

"Can Apryl check my right ear?" Jerico asked with a plaintive tone.

"Knock it off, Jerico!" Slade said to a *Hooyah!* from the full Team.

AMELIA EARHART SKYPORT—LAUNCH

We had gone through this exercise so often that the process had nearly become routine. Backed up by Senior Chief Bob Baxter, I kept a watchful eye on the guys to make sure that routine didn't cause them to miss something.

While the guys suited up, I descended to the lower level with Apryl. We gazed together through the large downward looking window. The skytower disappeared in the haze below us. Isolated swirling cloud formations filled the sky to the horizon in all directions. A storm was coming. Apryl wrapped her arms around my neck and kissed me softly.

"You come back to me, Sailor…you hear me?" She was near tears.

I held her close and whispered, "It's okay, Apryl. Nothing's going to happen."

"You don't know that," she said through tears that were now rolling down her cheeks. "It isn't just Mother Nature now. There's bad guys at the other end."

I kissed her tears away. "I know," I said softly. "I'll be careful, I promise."

She looked up at me, her blue eyes overflowing. "You better," she said and ran up the stairs.

✵

In a matter of minutes, the *Gryphon* team was suited up, including weapon battery backs, and both Rog and Slade were on their way down the rail, followed in short order by Jerico, Cappy, and Pete, while I was giving my *Gryphon* a final detailed check. The guys strapped me in and lowered my carapace cover. As the gantry hoisted me, I pushed Apryl's ministrations to the back of my mind and concentrated on the task at hand, which at the moment was the returning itch on my right buttock—obviously a psychological manifestation that accompanied my launches.

As I accelerated down the rail, picking up velocity for 1,300 klicks, I told myself, *Here you go again on a "we've never done this before" mission, and this time bad guys with weapons are waiting for us when we get there.*

SLINGSHOT RAIL

Routine is routine even if it is not precisely the same. Exactly four minutes and ten seconds after launch, Mother rotated my pallet 30° to the left. Thirty-two seconds later and 1,327 klicks down the rail, Mother released my pallet and initiated a two-minute-ten-second kick thruster burn. We headed away from the Earth at almost 8 km/s on a Hohmann Transfer Orbit (HTO) that passed 240 klicks to the north and 19 klicks above Fred Noonan Skyport, not that different from my first Squad drop. Apogee was over Lagos, Nigeria, as before, where I expected to meet the other five team members.

I relaxed into freefall and allowed myself to think about Apryl for a few minutes while we flew over the eastern Pacific and Mexico. As we approached the Atlantic south of Florida and the nighttime terminator, I began to give serious thought to exactly how we would carry out our mission once we descended through the nighttime sky over the Indian Ocean north of Madagascar.

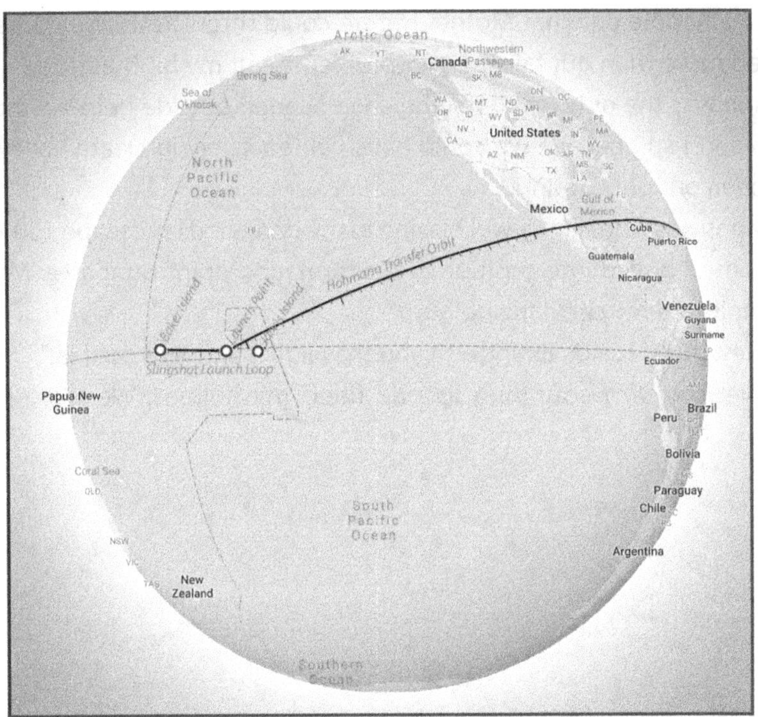

Slingshot Space Launch Loop with the Hohmann Transfer Orbit.

LEO

Unlike our first Squad drop where we traveled half-way around the world after our circularizing burn so that we could drop into southern Nevada, this time we would commence our drop seven minutes after we attained LEO. We would be over western Tanzania, just east of Lake Rukwa. At least, that was the plan Capt. Nelson and the Coronado team put together.

Mother was very good at bringing us together at apogee. I used to hover over her shoulder to make sure she got it right, but lately, I discovered I had better things to do. As I climbed higher along my HTO, while playing tag with my itch, I didn't bother with the grand view of the Earth below. I was too preoccupied with thinking up contingencies after the drop and finding their solutions. During our many orbital drops, we really had gotten a handle on what Mother Nature could throw at us. We had experienced more than our fair share of problems, but my high-altitude goose collision was the only incident where we needed outside help—although Jerico and I still believe we could have landed safely in Death Valley had that been our only option.

Lagos was a brilliant jewel blazing in the darkened landscape 160 klicks below me. I pulled into position at the formation point right after Mother accomplished my circularizing burn.

"Hey, guys," I said. "Extinguish your nav lights and let's do this!"

Five *Hooyahs!* sounding as one filled my helmet. We were ready to go.

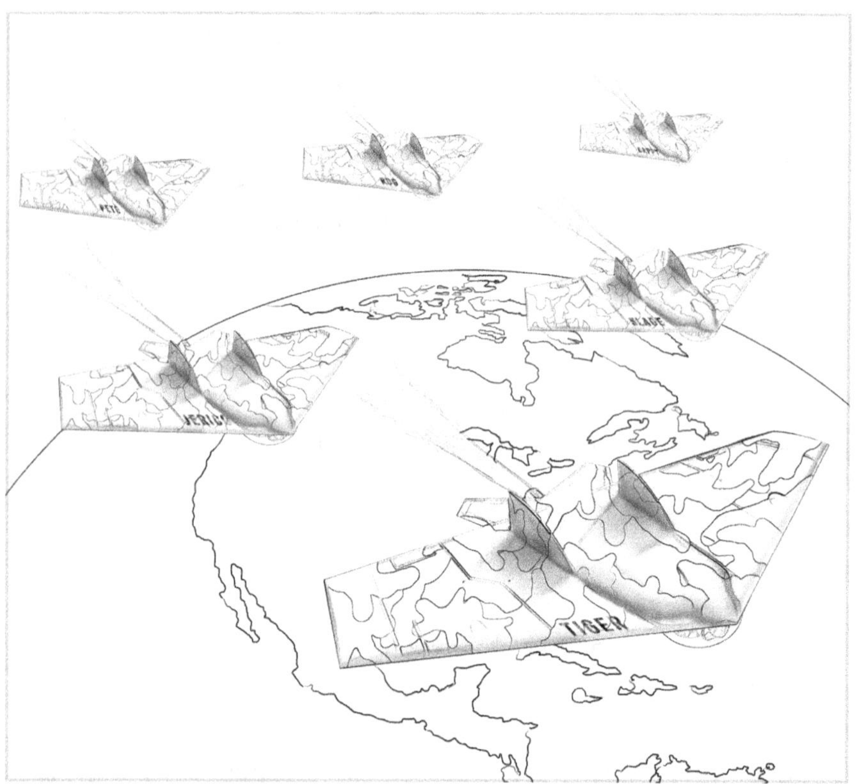

Tiger's SWIC team in LEO preparing for drop.

LEO—COMBAT DROP

As soon as I got into position at the tip of the formation, I ordered Mother to reverse our pallets in preparation for deorbiting. While Mother rotated the pallets with our gyros, I followed the process on my heads-up. I know I've said it before, but the display was as close to a video game as you can get—especially here in LEO.

"We drop in four minutes," I said. "Everybody good?" I was concerned because this was the first time that anybody had dropped from LEO into a combat scenario. My guys were Navy SEALS. There was no combat situation they couldn't handle, but this was so dramatically different from anything any warrior had ever done before, that I wanted assurance that my team members had no second thoughts.

I got five ragged *Hooyahs!* back—what else could I have expected?—and then Mother initiated the deorbiting burn.

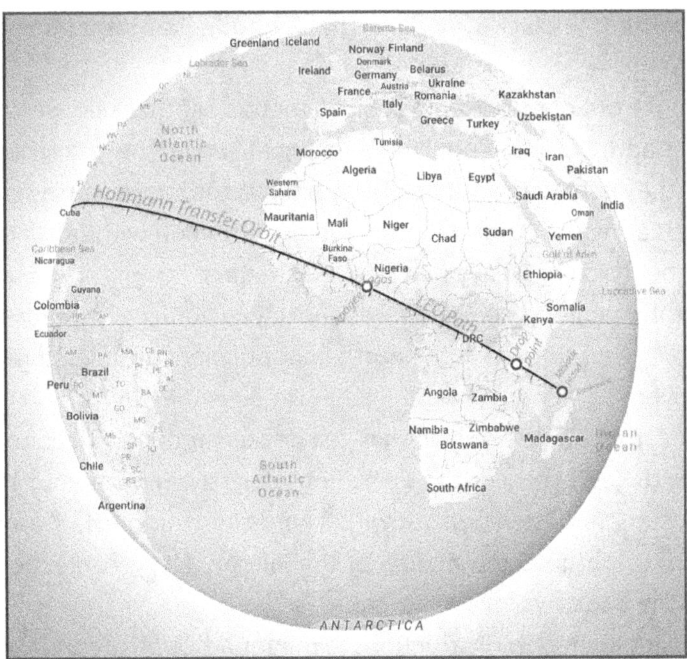

The Hohmann Transfer Orbit and the apogee with the shortened LEO path. The drop point and destination, Mayotte Island.

Mother cut our burn, rotated each of us so we were once again pointed in our direction of travel, and then she dropped our pallets. I felt a slight tug as my automatic, self-sealing oxygen connector broke away. About thirty seconds later, I watched five bright flashes from five pallets with their oxygen and hypergolic fuel tanks burning up in the nighttime atmosphere. I did not spot the sixth one before they plunged into the cloud layer.

Lake Rukwe lay about a hundred klicks off to our right, but it was too dark below us to see anything at all. A few minutes ahead on the coast was Mtwara. I vaguely remembered something about a failed groundnut export operation that was the reason for anything at all at this location. I don't think there's much there now. We were pretty busy skipping into and out of the atmosphere at that point, and I don't really remember if I saw any lights on the ground or not.

Besides, cloud cover obscured the surface every time we dipped down. Can you imagine what it's like at night, high over clouds, or dark jungle, or ocean? Nothing… black… nada… Thank goodness Mother knew where we were.

We broke out of our last dip at 8,000 meters. Mother said we were over Mayotte Island, but you could've fooled me. Above, the heavens were as bright as they ever were, but below lay a thick, turbulent storm system.

"Winds at five-thousand meters average fifty kph with gusts to ninety kph," Mother told us. "Heavy rain from 500 meters."

Control dropped the Mayotte Island layout onto my heads-up, pin-pointing *Platypus* docked at the north Longoni pier and briefed me on the fighter cover.

"Squad, this is Tiger. *Platypus* has just docked at the north Longoni pier, port side to. Pete, you cut the lines. Rog, push away with your bow and stern thrusters, and then pull out with a hard-right-rudder. Pull around the point to the right into the middle of the lagoon. Navy fighters overhead will keep the bad guys away from the ship."

After I completed my instructions to the squad, Control continued brief-ing me. "Tiger, the senator's family is still aboard *Platypus*. Senator Manfred has been relocated to a small reservoir about seven-and-a-half klicks in the hills southeast of Port Longoni. Mother will get you there. You will need to locate him, terminate his guards, and get to the clear extraction point on the hill to the northwest. We'll drop you a Fulton surface-to-air recovery system for the senator and two bladders of pressurized hypergolic fuel to get you and Jerico to your airborne extraction point."

Almost as an afterthought, Control added, "The pirates have made a one-hundred-million-dollar demand for the senator's safe return."

✷

"Listen up, everyone, this is Tiger," I said. "Drop down to a thousand meters. Watch the wind!"

"Tiger, this is Control. We just established contact with a *Platypus* crew member sequestered in the ship's forward chain locker. We described your wingsuits. He says you can land on each bridge wing and on the main deck just aft of the bow. He says the pirates are technically ignorant. A crew member had to sail and dock the ship for them. They have four men on board, one at the brow leading down to the dock, one in the Bridge, and two roaming guards. There's a fifth pirate roaming the dock."

"This is Tiger," I said. "Rog, make your assignments."

"This is Rog. Slade, take the starboard bridge wing—on your left as we fly in. Take out any bad guys in the bridge. I'll take the port and eliminate the brow guard. Cappy, land on the bow main deck, find those roaming guards and take them out. Pete, land on the dock near the bow. Take out the roving patrol, slice the mooring hawsers with your weapon, and get airborne ASAP. Any questions?"

He got three *Hooyahs!*

At a thousand meters, the wind was still a factor, but it seemed to be a steady blow from the ocean to the northeast, carrying a lot of rain. That was good for us—made us more difficult to spot, while we had Mother and our heads-up displays to guide us.

Rog and his guys dropped to 300 meters, setting up for the attack.

"On my six, Jerico!" I ordered as I vectored southeast and increased my descent rate as much as possible. Mother superimposed the terrain on my heads-up. The reservoir lay six klicks ahead, and beside it, between reservoir and extraction point, Senator Manfred's Link beacon flashed on my display.

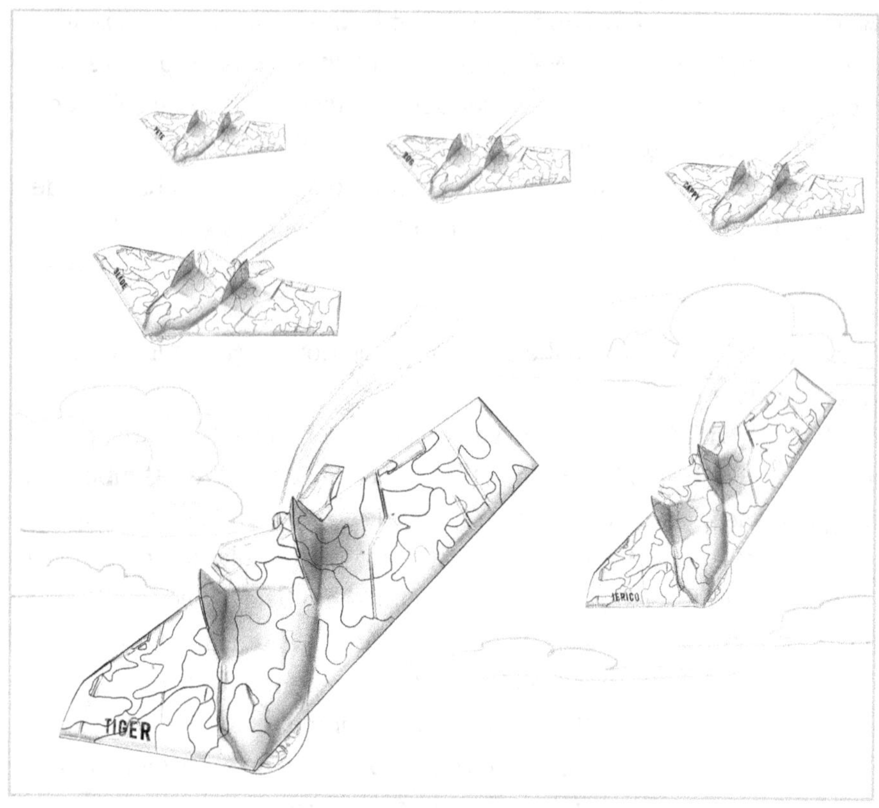

Rog and his team head to free CS Platypus.
Tiger and Jerico on their way to rescue Senator Manfred.

MAYOTTE ISLAND—*CS PLATYPUS*

While Jerico and I were occupied inland, Rog and his team dropped straight down through the rain to one hundred meters above the calm lagoon waters. They flew over the *Platypus*, dropped to fifty meters, and made a bow-on approach. The dock was brilliantly lit. Pete dropped stealthily to the bright dock, grabbed his silent energy pulse weapon as he left his *Gryphon*, and took out the three nearest lights and the roving guard who was half-way between the bow and brow, walking away from Pete. The guard never knew what hit him. Rog landed on the port bridge wing, stepped out of his *Gryphon* with his weapon and silently took out the guard at the brow three decks below him, and then he took out the two nearest dock lights. Simultaneously, Slade dropped to the starboard bridge wing, shed his *Gryphon*, and took out the unsuspecting bridge guard who had just turned to see what was happening on the port bridge wing. While this was happening, Pete ran along the dock burning through each hawser with a quick weapon burst. When he reached the last mooring, a bullet whizzed past his head. He turned, shot the pirate who had appeared on the road at the middle of the dock, and then he shot out the remaining dock light.

The prevailing wind had already pushed the *Platypus* away from the dock. Rog started the stern thruster and revved the main engines to full power. He threw the rudder hard right and willed the stern not to hit the dock.

Rog picked up the general announcing mike and said, "This is Lt. Roger Brook, U.S. Navy SEALS Winged Insertion Command. We have taken over this ship and eliminated most of the pirates. We are getting underway for Antsiranana, Madagascar. Please remain in your staterooms with your doors locked until I give you an *All Clear*."

Pete ran back toward his *Gryphon*, dodging several bullets as he ran. He returned fire at two of the flashpoints, without knowing if he got the shooters or not, and then he mounted his wingsuit and rocketed up into the driving rain.

Mother outlined *Platypus* in Pete's heads-up and then announced, "Incoming!" Before Pete had a chance to react, his rear-facing pulse weapon destroyed the incoming shoulder-fired missile. Pete raced over the north end of Longoni harbor to meet *Platypus* a kilometer into the broad lagoon. He came around to her bow, intending to land where Cappy had touched down earlier.

Still fifty meters out, as he dropped lower to land, a bright flash from below the bridge at the rear of the deck announced another missile launch. Before Pete had time to react, Mother aimed and fired his forward weapon, destroying the missile just three meters before impact. Cappy came out of the shadows and fired at the launch point of the missile. A pirate with a smoking hole in his chest fell forward out of the shadow.

Still twenty meters from the bow, Pete's rocket coughed and stopped, out of fuel. He set his wings for maximum glide, lifted his nose, and missing the bow by centimeters, landed softly on the darkened deck.

Suddenly, a shot rang out from the starboard side of the ship, hitting Cappy's right shoulder, spinning him around as he fell. Pete rolled out of his *Gryphon* while drawing his weapon and fired at the flashpoint just as Slade on the bridge wing above did the same. A loud scream filled the darkness as the last pirate stumbled out onto the main forward deck, left arm completely missing and his right shoulder mangled beyond recognition. When he saw the two SEALS, he shook his head in total disbelief and threw himself over the rail into the dark lagoon waters.

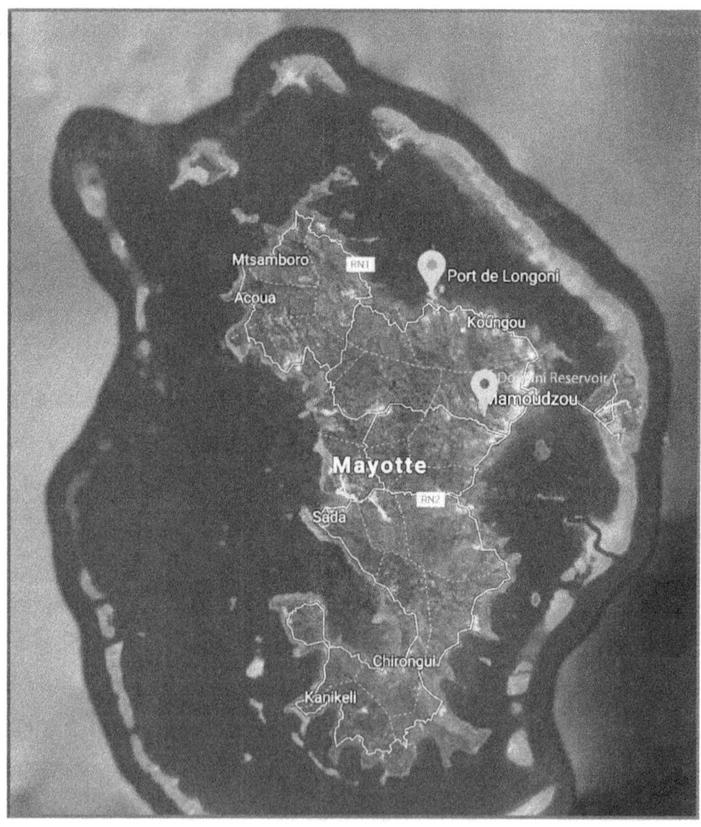

Mayotte Island with Port of Longoni and Doujani Reservoir

MAYOTTE ISLAND—DOUJANI RESERVOIR

It took about twenty minutes to get to Doujani Reservoir, using most of our remaining fuel. We landed silently in a narrow clearing about 250 meters to the northwest of and fifty meters above the reservoir. We exited the *Gryphons*, holstered our weapons, and discarded our helmets. My Link showed that Senator Manfred was down the slope in a clump of trees about twenty meters from the water's edge.

Wearing night-vision glasses, and getting soaked by the rain, Jerico and I crept to the edge of the slope. Mother was hooked into our Links. She superimposed the senator's exact position over our night vision view. I activated my infra-red sensor. Down by the water, four heat sources clumped together, and another was a couple of meters to the side. I slowly scanned a full circle around me. Other than a couple of obvious night critters, I saw nothing else.

I placed a finger to my lips and signaled Jerico to circle around to the left. I indicated I would circle right. I pointed to him, held up two fingers, and then slashed across my throat. I pointed at myself and indicated the same. He nodded.

I crept down the slope to my right, any sound I made muffled by the rain. Although I couldn't see Jerico, I knew he was doing the same to the left. We both reached the clump of trees with the Pirates and Manfred about five minutes later. We drew our weapons and aimed. Four energy bolts silently removed the heads of the hapless pirates. Senator Manfred's eyes got big as platters, but to his credit, he didn't utter a sound.

I stepped in front of the senator and whispered quietly, "Navy SEALS. Are there any other bad guys?"

He swallowed and shook his head, his eyes large with fright. I saw him make a conscious effort to quell his shaking hands. I gestured him to follow us. He did so silently, clearly aware of what was at stake. When we got to the clearing, I signaled Control.

"We have the senator. Ready to receive the Fulton system."

"Tiger, this is Randy Dorsey. I'm in a Herc a thousand meters overhead with several members of your SWIC team—Benny, Piggy, and

Cowboy—and a Fulton ready for a guided paradrop. I see your marker, but we are dealing with significant winds aloft. Your guys will remotely guide the Fulton down to the two-hundred-meter level. Then you take over. It has IR markers so you can see it with your night vision."

"I got it, Randy. Let her fly!"

Mother gave me a clear view in my glasses. The Fulton kept drifting to the west, but my SWIC team members in the Herc kept pulling it back overhead. At 200 meters, I took over, and as it got lower, the winds lessened. At seventy-five meters, I started to make out the four IR beacons, one at each corner. I eased the Fulton in and set it down just two meters from where we crouched.

I glanced over at the Senator. He seemed to have gotten his emotions under control. I knew from news reports that he was a man used to being in control. This had to be entirely outside his experience. "How are you holding up, Senator?" I asked.

He responded with a slight grin and shrugged shoulders. "This is way outside my MOS," he said quietly.

I lifted my eyebrows at his response. "Army Ranger," he said and gave me his old unit.

"Hooyah!" I responded as we exchanged high-fives.

"Any news on my family?" he asked.

"My guys took the ship," I told him. "they should be safe."

Jerico removed the fuel bladders from the pallet, and then set up the Fulton while I explained the next steps to the senator. Jerico handed him a harness. I showed him how to put it on.

"Jerico is inflating a helium balloon with a strong bungee line attached. We will attach the bungee line to your harness, and then you will stand facing that way." I pointed into the wind. "Jerico will let the balloon rise to two-hundred meters. Randy will fly a line of position in his C-130 at near stall speed toward the balloon and will snag the line with a yoke installed on his nose. You will go flying into the air where crew members will hook your line, and you will be reeled into the cargo hatch." I grinned at him. "It's like a super exciting amusement park ride."

He looked at me with a bit of a lopsided grin. "I've done a lot of things," he said, "but this will be a first." We exchanged another high-five.

We walked to where Jerico had rigged the blimp-shaped balloon.

"It's on its way to two hundred meters," Jerico said. "Let's get you hooked up." He securely attached the senator's harness to the bungee cord with two stainless carabiners. "You ready?" Jerico asked.

"I am." I could see his jaw set tightly.

"Gimme five!" Jerico held up his gloved hand.

DOUJANI RESERVOIR SNAG

I notified Dorsey that we were ready.

"Expect me in ten or less," Dorsey answered.

Seven minutes later, Senator Jack Manfred, former Army Ranger, ex-hostage, probable future U.S. President, whisked silently into the dark, rainy sky.

The Fulton ground-to-air extraction system

While we were waiting, Jerico had fueled our *Gryphons*. We donned our helmets, climbed into our wingsuits, and rocketed into the wet darkness.

"We're airborne, Randy. How's your passenger?"

"He's on board, none the worse for wear, and he expresses his thanks. Oh…and he talked with his wife. His family's safe."

"Tell him he can thank us in person in a few minutes," I said. "You got us on radar."

"'Sa fact," Dorsey said. "I'm doin' one-hundred-fifty, three hundred meters ahead of you."

"We're coming tandem," I said. "Jerico first. I'll be ten meters behind and ten below."

The open maw of the C-130 appeared out of the darkness in front of and a couple meters below us, its cargo bay brilliantly lit. Jerico dropped onto the ramp, cut his rocket, retracted his wings, and with one smooth move slid into the cargo bay. Dorsey dropped the Herc ten meters, and I set up to duplicate Jerico's maneuver.

At that moment, Mother interrupted with "Incoming!" She dropped my *Gryphon* several meters while simultaneously firing several bursts at the incoming missile from my rear weapon. The first two missed, but the third one struck the missile's rocket engine just a meter behind *my* nozzle. The missile disintegrated without exploding and fell back to earth.

"Okay, Tiger, let's try again," Dorsey said in his calm aviator's voice.

As I brought my *Gryphon* around to get into position, Mother again announced "Incoming!" She launched a volley at the missile, but before they affected it, the missile broke up in mid-air as it was struck by hundreds of rapid-fire .50 cal. bullets. Immediately thereafter, a large explosion enveloped the entire clearing that we had so recently vacated.

"That should simplify things," a new voice said on the circuit. "Lt. Joe 'Happy' Snider, U.S. Navy, at your service."

"Thanks, Happy, I owe you one. Tiger out!"

✷

My *Gryphon* ceased sliding along the Herc deck, and I secured my electronics and popped open my clamshell. As I swung to vertical, to my utter astonishment, I found myself wrapped in a tangle of female arms and legs.

"Tiger, Tiger…You're safe! You're safe!"

My helmet disappeared, and I experienced the most intense, tear-flooded liplock of my life. As I surfaced from its intensity, I began to hear laughter and cheering.

"Apryl…What the…How the hell did you get here?" I was genuinely mystified.

"She reached out to your command," Dorsey said, stepping into my view. "Somehow, they got her to Antsiranana in time to board my Herc—in her medical capacity, of course. She insisted that she knew you and your team medically better than anyone. Who was I to argue?"

MAYOTTE ISLAND—LAGOON

On board the *Platypus*, Pete did a quick field dressing on Cappy's shoulder. His spacesuit was shot, but that didn't matter. Cappy was alive and could function even though he was not a lefty.

On the bridge, Rog set his radar for close-in.

"Slade, watch the waters around us. We don't want a surprise boarding."

As they watched, twenty small craft departed Longoni Harbor, spotlights sweeping the water before them. "I'm getting underway," Rog said. "Get the others down on the main deck, ready to fire." He brought up the navigation system and pointed the cruise ship toward the nearest deep opening in the coral reef. Unlike a small craft, a large ship takes its time to build up speed, and Rog didn't want to move any faster than he thought he could handle through the slot in the reef.

As the watercraft closed the *Platypus*, the pirates commenced firing their small arms. "Hold fire until you are certain to be effective," Rog told his crew.

Suddenly, rapid-fire rained from above as two Navy fighters swept over the water between *Platypus* and the approaching small craft armada.

"This is Lt. Joe 'Happy' Snider and Lt. Bob 'Borax' Johnson, U.S. Navy, at your service! Tally Ho!"

Half the small craft floundered with the first pass. A second pass took out most of the remainder. As both fighters rose steeply into the night sky, a lone shoulder-fired missile chased them as they disappeared. The missile flamed out before it reached the clouds.

DAEDALUS COMBAT—FINALE

Rog turned out to be a pretty good ship handler. He successfully maneuvered *Platypus* out of Mayotte Lagoon and got underway for Antsiranana on Madagascar. The ship's doctor did a professional job on Cappy's shoulder. He was ready to party by the time *Platypus* reached port.

Jerico, Apryl, and I, along with Senator Manfred, arrived at Antsiranana International Airport a couple of hours after we successfully boarded Randy's Herc. Senator Manfred was whisked off by chopper to *Platypus* to see his family. The rest of the SWIC team refused to let us do anything. They serviced our *Gryphons* and wheedled out of us every detail of our pirate adventure. By the time we walked into the airport proper, the world media had arrived. We became the heroes of the hour and remained thus until Rog brought *Platypus* into the waters off Antsiranana. A pilot brought the ship to dock, and then the media forgot Jerico and me while they proceeded to court Rog and his guys—and rightly so. They were the ones who got shot up rescuing over 500 innocent passengers.

When the media learned that we had all dropped from LEO, except for Apryl, of course, who clung to me the entire time, the circus started all over again. It literally took us two days to extricate ourselves.

For a second time, we got to meet with the Commander-in-Chief. His personal friend and hand-picked successor, Senator Jack Manfred, was in the Oval Office with us. Rescuing him, saving his life, gave all of us special status with the Boss.

So, now the World knows about SWIC. It knows that Navy SEALS can appear absolutely anywhere at all, at any time. And that's a good thing.

PLEASE POST A REVIEW FOR DAEDALUS COMBAT

ON

AMAZON.COM AND GOODREADS.COM

I really appreciate you posting a review on Amazon and Goodreads. Posting to Amazon.com is intuitive. To post a review on Goodreads.com, go to their website, and become a member if you are not already one. Search for *Daedalus Combat*, and click on the "Want to read" button under the image of *Daedalus Combat*. Indicate that you have read *Daedalus Combat* and then you will be able to post a review. Thank you very much for going through this effort!

EXCERPT FROM: SLINGSHOT

by

Robert G. Williscroft

EQUATORIAL PACIFIC—SOUTHEAST OF BAKER ISLAND

Margo stopped kicking her feet as the ominous gray shapes flashed into her peripheral view. Long, tawny hair floated past her head as her feet dropped below her slim, brightly clad body. She took a deep breath and floated slightly upward. A hint of fear crept into her mind as she turned toward three gray, sleek predators cruising just inside the limit of her vision, about twenty-five meters away.

A gentle touch on her shoulder startled her. She turned to see Alex Regent tapping the depth reading on his dive-console with his index finger. Margo reached down and grasped her console, turning it so she could read her depth: twenty-five meters. She had drifted upward five meters since seeing the sharks.

Margo exhaled angrily and let some air out of her breathing bag. She knew better than to lose track of her depth. Out there, her life depended on a constant awareness of exactly how deep she was. Together she and Alex sank back to thirty meters. Off to their right, the three gray shapes drifted with them. Would she ever get used to it, she thought, as she released a bit of air into her bag to stop her descent.

"Alex," she said.

There was no response.

"Alex!" She tapped the back of her console several times.

"Alex!" Nothing but silence.

Alex placed himself in front of Margo and looked into her facemask. With his right hand, he formed a circle with thumb and forefinger. His three other fingers extended straight up.

Margo returned the sign indicating she was all right while nodding vigorously. Then she pointed to her ear and lifted her console, tapping the back. Alex fumbled at his ear and then tapped his console, and then shook his head.

Great, Margo thought, *EFCom is busted just when we really need it. Not busted,* she corrected herself, *just a submerged antenna.* She pointed to the three menacing shapes off to her right. Alex turned and scanned around them. Above and just behind them the blue-painted hull of their boat bobbed in the gentle waves. About twenty meters ahead of them hung a smooth, horizontal fluorescent orange tube about one meter in diameter. To the left, it stretched into the gloom; to the right, it angled downward. The fluorescent tube was attached to a slender cable angling up to the shadow of a buoy just beneath the surface to their right. Alex turned back toward Margo, making an exaggerated shrug.

Margo reached for her dive-console again and pressed a button located prominently on its face. The three sharks turned and commenced a meandering movement toward the two divers. Their front fins extended stiffly downward at about forty-five degrees. Their backs arched slightly, and their blunt snouts moved back and forth as they approached.

Margo felt her hair stand up on the nape of her neck. She turned to Alex and motioned him to her side. Alex withdrew a telescoped baton from its holder at his waist and extended it to its full one-and-a-half-meter length. He checked the safety lever near its handle, and with his thumb he flicked the lever so it pointed forward. As the sharks drew nearer, he held the stick out in front of him, pointed in their direction. Margo glanced around them again and pushed her console button once more. Alex waved the stick about slowly and then steadied up on the nearest of the three menacing monsters.

Suddenly, with blurring speed, the nearest shark attacked. Alex struck out with his stick, the jolt of its impact rocking him backward. A sharp crack was followed by a hissing sound as carbon dioxide rushed into the shark's body. In the same moment, flashes of silvery-black streaked from several directions. One of the remaining sharks was struck broadside by a dolphin's blunt nose. In a flash, it disappeared.

The animal Alex had injected rolled on its side and began a crazed, uncontrolled spiral toward the surface thirty meters above them. On its way up, it was hit several times by charging dolphins. It expired of massive embolisms before reaching fifteen meters. In the melee, the third shark vanished.

Margo reached out for Alex, grabbed a handful of breathing bag, and pulled him close to her. She placed the flat of her full-facemask against his and looked deeply into his eyes, as close to a kiss as she could come under the circumstances. Even down here, they were deep blue. Several bubbles escaped from the positive pressure maintained inside their masks and shimmered their way toward the surface, expanding rapidly as they rose.

Like an old-time scuba diver, Margo thought, watching the rising silvery spheres. Instinctively she checked the volume in her breathing bag and glanced at the gauge on her tiny, ultra-high-pressure air flask. She found she was holding her breath, and as she felt the need to breathe, a gentle pressure developed against her back. She pulled back and turned to confront a two-and-a-half-meter-long dolphin nudging her from behind.

It was one of four that had responded to her sonic signal—George, her favorite. The other three dolphins crowded in around the neoprene and nylon suited divers, jostling each other for attention. Margo rubbed the head dome of each and indicated to Alex that he should do the same. Then the two of them turned their attention back to the tube suspended in front of them.

Alex swam to the angled portion and began to search along the tube's length, descending slowly. Margo dropped her arm from George's neck and kicked in Alex's direction, keeping him in sight, but staying between him and the surface. The four cetaceans arrowed toward the surface and grabbed a gulp of air, then settled back down, playfully cycling between Alex and Margo, gently jostling them. About thirty minutes later, Alex motioned Margo to join him. She released a bubble of air from her bag and dropped down beside him. Her console showed a depth of fifty meters. Alex pointed to a five-centimeter rip in the bottom curve of the tube's fluorescent covering.

Margo reached into a deep pocket located on the left leg of her suit and withdrew a role of patching tape. Alex stretched the edges of the tear, and Margo applied a strip of self-sealing tape along the opening. Then she located a small pneumatic valve on the top of the tube and attached a hose from her spare air tank. On a signal from Alex, she released air into the tube, forcing water out through a one-way valve on the underside. She stopped when bubbles escaped from the lower valve.

As the tube rose slowly, Margo held on, keeping track of their progress on her console. They stopped rising when the gauge read thirty meters. Margo felt the tube—it was taut and solid. She tapped the back of her console, listening for the faint rush of sound in her ears. Nothing. She pointed to the back of her console and then her ear, and shook her head. Alex offered another of his exaggerated underwater shrugs and grinned, although the only part of the grin she could see was his crinkled eyes. She grinned back and pointed toward the suspension buoy and their boat, making an angled upward sign with her free hand. Alex nodded, checked his console, and they both headed back, slowly rising as they swam.

Margo saw Alex check his console from time to time, making certain they kept below the ever-changing ceiling limit it calculated for him. Since she had remained shallower than Alex for most of the dive, she knew she would be safe following his lead. She looked around at the four dolphins. Her earlier fright was gone, and she simply enjoyed George's protective nearness and the playful bumps and nudges from the others.

On the surface finally, Alex dropped his facemask down around his neck, fully inflated his bag and grinned at Margo. "Close call down there!"

Margo shoved her facemask down and patted the glistening snout that appeared in front of her. "Thanks, George. I love you too."

The dolphin mewed a pleased response, lifted his body out of the water and backed away, chattering as he went. The other three animals circled at and below the surface, keeping watch over their human charges.

"What happened to the EFCom?" Margo asked. "I expected it to come back online as soon as the antenna surfaced."

"Broken antenna wire, I imagine," Alex answered.

"Storm damage, I'm sure," said Margo, as they turned and headed toward the waiting vessel.

"Probably," agreed Alex. "But that wasn't a burst seam," he added.

"Yeah, maybe the sinking tube snapped the wire."

Actually, tube flotation chambers flooded on a regular basis. They had patched a full ten percent of them since the project started. But it was a bit unusual to find a rip on the tube bottom, and the Electrostatic Field Communication ("EFCom") transceivers on the buoys almost always survived.

✵

The EFCom buoy nearest the tear had ceased transmitting, and the buoys on either side of the tear had signaled their departure from datum a day earlier. Alex had opted to employ an electrostatic field communication system, because of its clear underwater signal transmission capability that was independent of acoustic conditions, since it didn't rely on sound transmission through the water. Every buoy, each skimmer and floater, and every diver was outfitted with one of the small EFCom transceivers. Alex had inspected the non-transmitting buoy personally during an overflight from Jarvis Island. There was nothing visible on the two kilometers of surface between the buoys; they were closer together, but not so that it was visible to the eye. Nevertheless, the remaining 1,828-odd buoy-suspended kilometers of tube were stressing from the downward pull of the waterlogged section. The buoy near the tear was several meters underwater.

Suspended inside the flotation tube were two virtually impervious, lightweight, hose-like tubes, each about six centimeters in diameter, called vacuum sheaths. Two shallow channels jutted out from the bottom of each vacuum sheath, filled with electronically-controlled suspending magnets. Magnetically suspended inside each vacuum sheath was a five-centimeter tube of segmented soft iron officially called the rotor, but more popularly known as the ribbon, so named from the earliest conceptions back in the 1980s of the Launch Loop inventor, Keith Lofstrom. Alex was eager to check continuity readings to make certain the vacuum sheaths had not breached. They were not yet evacuated, but seawater entry at this stage would seriously delay the entire project. If the EFCom had not crapped out, the tests would already be underway.

Alex glanced ahead at Margo Jackson, cavorting with her four dolphins as they made their leisurely way back to the waiting boat. His field engineer in charge of underwater construction was a remarkable female. Nearly as tall as his own 183 centimeters, her model's slender figure, encased in electric-blue nylon-covered neoprene, seemed to lack feminine curves. He knew differently, of course, having joined her bikini-clad person from time to time for morning swims since the project began over two years ago.

The project—Alex had lived with it for three years before actual construction began. Longer, actually, if you considered dreams—since before the incredible, worldwide bi-millennial celebration when he still was a young boy.

There was the nearly simultaneous publication in America and England of practically identical ideas in 1985. Paul Birch published an article in *The Journal of the British Interplanetary Society*, while in America Keith Lofstrom published his article in a supplement to *The Journal of the Astronautical Sciences*, he recalled. Nobody could agree on the names: Skyrail, Launch Loop, Beanstalk. There were others, but the idea is what counted, the sky-shaking idea that you don't need rockets to get into space.

Newspapers were full of explanations three-and-a-half years ago when the aging president of a computer software giant made the announcement. He would funnel a significant portion of company profits into the consortium. Space travel would become as commonplace and inexpensive as the personal computers his pioneering work had made possible. He went on to outline the easy-to-understand concept.

Imagine a water hose streaming water in a parabolic arch. Deflect the water and funnel it back to the start through a pump, creating a closed system. Make the stream strong enough and the hose light enough, and the entire structure will support itself—the water holding up the hose structure. Now, replace the water with a thin, closed-loop pipe of segmented soft iron. Make it 5,000 kilometers around and accelerate it to orbital velocity with gigantic linear induction motors from two points on the equator 2,000 kilometers apart. The center section of the structure, including both the outgoing and return legs of the loop, will rise to about eighty kilometers above the Earth. Supply access to the upstream end in space with a Kevlar-hung elevator, and you can launch capsules by magnetically coupling them to the rapidly moving pipe of iron.

Slingshot, they called it. The greatest engineering undertaking in the history of the world, they said.

As the on-scene project manager, Alex was responsible for getting the job done, on schedule, on budget. He was building a gossamer structure over 2,500 kilometers long, a frail spider web, completely invisible when viewed from more than a few kilometers. Alex grinned wryly. All *Slingshot* really consisted of was a fancy evacuated tube, a flexible iron pipe, four linear drivers and their power sources, some guy wires, and a couple of elevators. Put that way it seemed simple enough. But, of course, it wasn't simple at all, and for all his skill and engineering competence, and despite surface appearances, deep down Alex was not entirely sure that he could make it happen.

Margo and Alex climbed up the ladder and onto *Skimmer One's* bobbing fantail. This was one of two skimmers on the project—twelve-meter-long surface-effect boats that looked more like a floating aircraft than a traditional motorboat. They were capable of 200 knots, skimming about one-and-a-half meters over the wave tops. They had a small open fantail, just large enough for a couple of divers to doff their gear. Being on the fantail when the skimmer was on its cushion was more than dangerous, and was strictly prohibited throughout the project.

Alex signaled to the waiting coxswain, and they got underway for Baker, plowing through the water while Alex and Margo remained exposed. He and Margo stood near the stern railing and removed their dripping skins. Alex looked back at the buoys, now presumably in their proper places.

"How many more times?" Alex looked quizzically at Margo.

"Who knows?" She glanced back at the bobbing buoys. "We have repair people available at both ends. We shouldn't be doing this ourselves, you know." She turned and looked directly at Alex. "What do you think—weather or sabotage?"

Alex shrugged and tossed the spent carbon dioxide cartridge from his shark stick in the general direction of the cavorting dolphins. "I wanted to see for myself, and I still don't know. Does it matter? We can't patrol the entire eighteen-hundred-twenty-eight-kilometer length anyway."

"What are we dealing with?" Margo asked. "You don't get out here in a rowboat."

"We're two thousand wet klicks from any kind of civilization," Alex said. "At minimum, that's a large motor-yacht or even an ocean sailer—you know, one of those we maybe can afford when this job is done." He sighed. "We're dealing with lots of money and someone with a major bitch."

He looked into her green eyes.

"Just keep my tubes at depth." His blue eyes flashed, and he turned toward the cockpit to radio his orders to test pipe continuity.

❋

Margo dropped her eyes at his challenge. For the thousandth time, she asked herself if she had bitten off more than she could chew with this assignment. Was it her fault that the flotation chambers kept ripping? Was she missing something important? Was she copping out to imply there might have been sabotage? And yet, Alex seemed to agree that it might be sabotage. When she joined the project two years ago, the newspapers had acclaimed her as the ideal role model for the new twenty-first-century woman. At times that burden lay heavily on her shoulders, as it did now, she reflected.

It was a vast responsibility, and there was no way one person actually could control all of it at once. How Alex handled the weight of the entire project awed her, but she was careful never to let him know.

Margo watched Alex step into the cockpit. He was tall and slender, richly tanned from his constant outdoor work. She felt a softness well up inside her, a gentle warmth spreading out from the pit of her stomach. She bit her lower lip and turned angrily to lean on the after-railing.

None of that, she chided herself. This assignment was too important, and the stakes too high, to let any kind of emotion intrude. As she entered the cabin and sealed the port, the skipper switched modes, and pressurized air quickly filled the hard-sided skirt. In moments the skimmer lifted out of the water, except for the port and starboard skirts that protruded about a meter into the waves. Within seconds, high-pressure water nozzles jetted water from the end of each skirt, and within thirty seconds *Skimmer One* was approaching 200 knots.

As *Skimmer One* headed into the afternoon sun, trailing an arrow-straight wake of white foam, Margo stood looking aft through the sealed port, remembering her instinctive sharing, and their underwater kiss following the fright of nearly becoming shark food. She shook off the sensation and busied herself with putting away their diving equipment. But a hint of a smile remained on her lips as they shot over the surface, finally settling back onto the water as they entered the small protected artificial harbor on the west side of Baker Island, just south of a shallow reef that went dry at low tide.

You have just been reading from Chapter One
of Slingshot, the 1st book in ***The Starchild*** *Trilogy,*
Robert Williscroft's exciting Science Fiction trilogy.

WORDS OF PRAISE FOR SLINGSHOT

Slingshot does for the launch loop what Arthur C. Clarke's *The Fountains of Paradise* or Sheffield's *Web Between the Worlds* did for the space elevator. Again, Williscroft delivers a great mix of hard science fiction and action.

— Alastair Mayer
Author of the *T-Space Series*

Robert Williscroft deftly crafts an energetic story around a phenomenal technological development just over the horizon: the space launch loop. The technical detail woven into this story is an education unto itself. But don't assume that Williscroft chooses raw infodump over story—*Slingshot* is an adventure that pulls you in, gives you characters that are engaging, and invites you to follow them through their challenges. What Williscroft has done in *Slingshot* is no easy task—he has balanced the *hard* aspect of science fiction with the character portrayals that those who despise that very *hard* science fiction beg for. The last decade has seen impressive leaps in the theoretical work toward the launch loop—this book couldn't come too soon! And you won't be able to keep from reading all the way to the end. Williscroft's art continues to be praise-worthy!

— Jason D. Batt, *100 Year Starship*
Author of *The Tales of Dreamside series*

I've been a fan of Robert Williscroft's books for a while now. They're action-packed and filled with all kinds of interesting, real-world information. *Slingshot* fits right in.

Slingshot is about the development of an earth-bound spaceport in which spaceships are taken 80 kilometers above the Earth by elevator and hurled onto their trajectory by a very fast-moving ribbon of soft iron. It is much easier, cheaper, and cleaner to launch spaceships from here due to the rarified atmosphere. This concept may be a reality someday. The book begins with a foreword by Keith Lofstrom, the originator of this concept called the "launch loop."

Learning about the launch loop is the most interesting aspect of this novel. Williscroft's descriptions of the construction techniques, its operations, and the benefits for space travel are absolutely fascinating. The book takes place about thirty years in the future, and I could easily see such a project becoming a reality in that time.

The plot of the novel is driven by the development and construction of the project, which is being threatened by ill-informed environmentalists bent on destroying the project. The launch loop is far greener than the current method of launching vehicles into space, but a sinister power has misled the environmentalists into believing that sabotaging the launch loop is saving the planet. Meanwhile, the sinister power is protecting its own economic interests.

As usual, Williscroft has created a cast of interesting and driven characters. The book is a fascinating read, and you are guaranteed not only to learn a lot, but to dream about the future of space travel.

— Marc Weitz, Past President
The Los Angeles Adventurers' Club

ABOUT THE AUTHOR

Dr. Robert G. Williscroft served twenty-three years in the U.S. Navy and the National Oceanic and Atmospheric Administration (NOAA). He commenced his service as an enlisted nuclear Submarine Sonar Technician in 1961, was selected for the Navy Enlisted Scientific Education Program in 1966, and graduated from University of Washington in Marine Physics and Meteorology in 1969. He returned to nuclear submarines as the Navy's first Poseidon Weapons Officer. Subsequently, he served as Navigator and Diving Officer on both catamaran mother vessels for the Deep Submergence Rescue Vehicle. Then he joined the Submarine Development Group One out of San Diego as the Officer-in-Charge of the Test Operations Group, conducting "deep-ocean surveillance and data acquisition"—which forms the basis for his Cold War novel *Operation Ivy Bells*.

In NOAA Dr. Williscroft directed diving operations throughout the Pacific and Atlantic. As a certified diving instructor for both the National Association of Underwater Instructors (NAUI) and the Multinational Diving Educators Association (MDEA), he taught over 3,000 individuals both basic and advanced SCUBA diving. He authored four diving books, developed the first NAUI drysuit course, developed advanced curricula for mixed gas and other specialized diving modes, and developed and taught a NAUI course on the Math and Physics of Advanced Diving. His doctoral dissertation for California Coast University, *A System for Protecting SCUBA Divers from the Hazards of Contaminated Water* was published by the U.S.

Department of Commerce and distributed to Port Captains worldwide. He also served three shipboard years in the high Arctic conducting scientific baseline studies, and thirteen months at the geographic South Pole in charge of National Science Foundation atmospheric projects.

Dr. Williscroft has written extensively on terrorism and related subjects. He is the author of a popular book on current events published by Pelican Publishing: *The Chicken Little Agenda—Debunking Experts' Lies*, now in its second edition as an eBook, and a new children's book series, *Starman Jones*, in collaboration with Dr. Frank Drake, world-famous director of the Carl Sagan Center for the Study of Life in the Universe and the SETI Institute.

Dr. Williscroft's 1st novel in *The Starchild Trilogy, Slingshot*, tells the story of the construction of the world's first Space Launch Loop. *Slingshot* was launched at the Seattle International Space Elevator Conference in August 2015. His 2nd novel in *The Starchild Trilogy, The Starchild Compact,* is based on the discovery that Saturn's moon Iapetus is actually a derelict starship, and how Earth explorers eventually meet with the "Founders," who originally arrived on the starship and populated the Earth long ago. The 3rd book in *The Starchild Trilogy, The Iapetus Federation*, the Federation expands Solar Systemwide, while a new Caliphate sweeps Earth. The Starchild Institute creates wormhole portals to enable the Exodus. Earth becomes medieval, while human focus shifts to the Iapetus Federation. Humans settle every potentially habitable spot in the Solar System and begin expanding into the rest of the Galaxy.

The SWIC Daedalus Files takes place in the world of *Slingshot*. In four short stories, *Daedalus*, *Daedalus LEO*, *Daedalus Squad*, and *Daedalus Combat*, Dr. Williscroft follows the U.S. Navy SEALS Winged Insertion Command (SWIC) and its development of the *Gryphon* hard wingsuit for combat drops from Low Earth Orbit

Dr. Williscroft is an active member of the venerable Adventurers' Club of Los Angeles, where he is the former Editor of the Club's monthly magazine. He is a board member of the Colorado Authors' League. He lives in Centennial, Colorado, with his wife, Jill, whom he met upon his return from the South Pole in 1982 and finally married in 2011, and their twin college boys (when they are home from school).

OTHER WORKS BY ROBERT G. WILLISCROFT

Please visit Amazon.com to discover other eBooks by Robert Williscroft and your favorite online or Brick & Mortar bookseller for their paper versions:

Current events:

The Chicken Little Agenda—Debunking "Experts'" Lies

Children's books:

The Starman Jones Series:

Starman Jones: A Relativity Birthday Present

Starman Jones Goes to the Dogs (scheduled for release in 2019)

Short Stories:

The SWIC Daedalus Files:

Daedalus

Daedalus—LEO

Daedalus—Squad

Daedalus—Combat

Novels:

Mac McDowell Missions:

Operation Ivy Bells

Operation Snow Cone (Scheduled for release 2020)

The Starchild Trilogy:

Slingshot
The Starchild Compact
The Iapetus Federation

The Oort Chronicles:

Icicle—A Tensor Matrix (scheduled for release in 2019)
The Oort—Interstellar Consequences (scheduled for release in 2020)
Oort Andromeda—Galactic Diaspora (scheduled for release in 2020)

CONNECT WITH ROBERT G. WILLISCROFT

I really appreciate you reading my book! Here are my social media coordinates:

Friend me on Facebook: *https://www.facebook.com/robert.williscroft*
Follow me on Twitter: *@RGWilliscroft*
Like my Amazon author page: *http://www.amazon.com/Robert-G.-Williscroft/e/B001JP52AS*
Subscribe to my blog: *http://thrawnrickle.com/*
Connect on LinkedIn: *http://www.linkedin.com/in/argee/*
Visit my website: *https://robertwilliscroft.com*

DAEDALUS COMBAT GLOSSARY

AFRICOM—American centralized military command and control for the African continent.

Baker Compound—The *Slingshot* facility on Baker Island.

BatCap—Power source for the Pulsed Energy Weapon, a unique marriage of a 3-D battery and a thin, large-surface-area flexible capacitor that the SWIC member wears on his back. The capacitor supports twenty rapid-release lethal laser bursts and recharges in less than a minute from the 3-D battery, or it can continuously support a lethal laser burst every five seconds. The 3-D battery needs recharging every five thousand bursts.

CS Platypus—*Cruise Ship Platypus*

EMT—Emergency Medical Technician.

Fulton—A surface-to-air extraction system developed in the 1950s. It involves using a harness and a self-inflating balloon with an attached lift line. A C-130-type aircraft engages the line with a V-shaped yoke on its nose, and the person is reeled on board.

Gryphon-7—A wingsuit-like carapace strapped on the body. It stopped short of the feet, but in flight could extend to a full two meters, stretching beyond the feet. It attached to the legs and arms, with special controls for each hand, and had a broad Velcro band across the midriff. It had extensible delta wings with a three-meter wingspan. The back end contained a small steerable hypergolic rocket engine, and the left and right wings each contained pressurized hypergolic fuel components. Switches in the hand units controlled the fuel valves. The *Gryphon* had a heads-up display with height-over-ground, airspeed, groundspeed, compass, and GPS coordinates superimposed on a map, plus various system readouts.

Gryphon-10—Like *Gryphon-7* with some radical changes including full body armor with circulating fuel for heat protection, an increased surface area using dimples, wrinkles, and rolls that dramatically boosted heat shedding, and it incorporated a new type of polymer that was stronger, lighter, and more heat resistant than anything before. The biggest change was Mother, the guidance computer unit designed to act on its calculations before the human pilot was even aware of them. Still man-transportable, although more ungainly than *Gryphon-7*. Its unpowered glide ratio was 14-1, and it could fly 100 level klicks under power.

Gryphon-10, Mk 4—Looked exactly like the *Gryphon-10*. It differed in subtle ways because of improvements developed during several LEO drops. Incorporated the latest model of a very efficient, hand-held, pulsed energy weapon into a node in the leading edge of either the left or right wing. Its power source is a lightweight BatCap. Before opening the carapace after landing, the SWIC member retrieves the weapon from its node and holsters it just like a sidearm.

Gryphon-10, Mk 5—Exactly like the *Gryphon-10, Mk 4*, except for the addition of a rear firing pulsed energy weapon.

Howland Island—A coral island in the equatorial Pacific about sixty-five kilometers north of Baker Island. It was the destination of Amelia Earhart when she disappeared.

HP oxygen—High-pressure oxygen

Hypergolic fuel– Fuel that ignites spontaneously when the individual fuel elements come into contact.

Hypergolic rocket or jet– A rocket or jet that uses hypergolic fuel.

Keith Lofstrom—Inventor of the Launch Loop.

Kick thruster—A small, reigniteable solid-state rocket attached to a capsule, used for vector changes after release from the rail, or to slow down a capsule used to transit from Baker to Jarvis. The rocket was extinguished with an iris-like very strong magnetic field that sliced through the solid fuel column just above the burn.

Klick—Slang word for kilometer.

Launch Loop—A means for getting into space without using rockets. Consists of a segmented soft iron ribbon moving at orbital speed, starting at ground level, elevating itself to 80 km, following the Earth's curvature for 1,800 km, returning to ground level, and then tracing the path back forming a continuous loop. Two elevator-equipped skytowers extend from the ground to the loop. At the top are two skyports at 80 km altitude. Personnel capsules and cargo pallets are magnetically coupled to the moving loop and launched into space.

Launch Loop International—The company that and manages Slingshot.

Launch pouch—Attaches to the capsule underside, enabling magnetic acceleration of the capsule up the skytower or by the rail.

LEO—Low Earth Orbit

Mach number—The ratio of the speed of a body to the speed of sound in the surrounding medium.

Mayotte Island—A small island northwest of Madagascar that has the largest coral-reef enclosed lagoon of any island in the world.

MOS—Military Occupation Specialty

Mother—A synchronized guidance computer across all units in an operation that was designed to act on its calculations before the human pilots were even aware of them..

Nitrogen tetroxide—A hypergolic fuel component (see UDMH).

Pallet—A regular cargo pallet used to transport cargo up the skytower and along the rail for launch into orbit. Each of these pallets carried four tanks. Two were HP oxygen used by the flyer until *Gryphon* separation, attached to the wingsuit with breakaway connectors. The other two carried hypergolic fuel, UDMH and nitrogen tetroxide, for the small hypergolic maneuvering jets

Pulsed Energy Weapon—Fires pulsed high-energy laser bursts. Is virtually silent.

Rail—Common term for the portion of the launch loop between the skyports.

Ribbon—Common term for the soft-iron tube that is the heart of the launch loop.

SEAL—An acronym for *Sea Air and Land*; a member of a Naval Special Warfare unit trained for unconventional warfare.

Skyport—The structure at the top of the skytower.

Skyrail—An alternative name for a Space Elevator or Launch Loop.

Skytower—The elevator-like set of cables that extends from the Skyport to the socket below.

Slingshot—The Space Launch Loop between Baker and Jarvis Islands in the equatorial Pacific.

Socket—The attachment point at the bottom of the skytower.

SWIC—SEALS Winged Insertion Command

UDMH—Unsymmetrical dimethylhydrazine, a hypergolic fuel component (see nitrogen tetroxide).

UV light—Ultraviolet light.

Wingsuit -Aa suit with fabric filling the gaps between stretched out arms and ankles, and between the legs, enabling the wearer to glide through the air.

THE DAEDALUS FILES

www.ingramcontent.com/pod-product-compliance
Lightning Source LLC
Chambersburg PA
CBHW070454170726
48291CB00005B/1743